Between The Lines

A Poetry Anthology

Autumn Acosta, Rachel M. Adams, Sana Baig, Jaela Deming, Anna Kailin Fletcher, Autumn Grace, Alladene Grace Hadden, Evelyn Harwood, Hazel Honegger, Ava Hope, Blessing Hope, Erin Hylands, Lissie Laws, Leighton Opperman, Margaret Pierce, Skylar Rivers, Owen Leo Snook, Jessica Sprecher, Emily Sweeney, and Cadence E. Witt

Featuring a poem by Kanasy Yeager

This is a work of fiction. Names, characters, places, and incidents either are the product of the author's imagination or are used fictitiously. Any resemblance to actual persons, living or dead, events, or locales is entirely coincidental.

Copyright 2024 by Autumn Acosta, Rachel M. Adams, Sana Baig, Jaela Deming, Anna Kailin Fletcher, Autumn Grace, Alladene Grace Hadden, Evelyn Harwood, Hazel Honegger, Ava Hope, Blessing Hope, Erin Hylands, Lissie Laws, Leighton Opperman, Margaret Pierce, Skylar Rivers, Owen Leo Snook, Jessica Sprecher, Emily Sweeney, Cadence E. Witt, and Kanasy Yeager.

All rights reserved. No part of this publication may be reproduced, stored or transmitted in any form or by any means, electronic, mechanical, photocopying, recording, scanning, or otherwise without written permission from the publisher. It is illegal to copy this book, post it to a website, or distribute it by any other means without permission.

Copyright © 2024
Edited by Erin Hylands
Interior Formatting by Rachel M. Adams
Cover Design by Lori Scharf
Published by Skillful Pen Press

Dedicated to Kanasy Yeager. Your light and love in the midst of pain is a reminder for us all that God's not done with us. We miss you, friend, and we eagerly await the day we can meet you in Heaven.

We thank you, Kanasy, for your beautiful words, and for this poem we share here.

Quietly Blessed
By Kanasy Yeager

I sit quietly in my room,
Thinking of all I have lost:
Strength,
Time,
A limb.
I'm blessed,
For I have not lost
Love,
Family,
Friends,
Hope.
My faith is stronger than before,
For when all was dark,
He held my hand.
I have no need to falter,
He pulled me close;
I learned to trust Him more,
For He has a plan,
Tho' I know it not.
He knows my limits;
He loves me still.
For all these things,
I shall sing,
I will shout
From the hilltops:
I am so blessed!

Between The Lines

A Poetry Anthology

Skillful Pen Press

Table of Contents

Introduction	13
A Call To Adventure	15
A Friend's Agony	17
America!	18
Another Funeral?	20
A Petition	22
A Prayer	24
Beauty For Ashes	25
Chiastic Lies	26
Come To Jesus	27
Conflicted	28
Consider It All Joy	29
Courage.	30
Darkness Is In Vain	31
Dearest Friend	32
Death Defeated	34
Despair the Messengers	35
Dross	36
Eclipsed	37
Falling	39
Flame	40
Friendship	41
Heartsong	43
Heavenly Maze	44
History	45
Hold On Tight	49

Hopeful or Hopeless	51
Hope in Five Senses	52
I Can't	53
Jasmine	55
Joy	56
Keilah	57
Lies	58
Moonlight Dawning	61
My King	65
My Turntable	67
Narrow Route	68
Next Steps	69
Oblivious	70
Once I Looked Up	72
Overwhelm	74
Perfect Storm	76
Reassurance	77
Refuge	78
Resilience	80
Shades	81
She Looked Back	82
Silence	84
Sometimes	86
Surrender	88
Tears	89
The Seashell	90
The Storm	91
The Whole World Is In Your Hands	93

This is Reconciliation	95
This Monster	96
Tirade	98
Violets	99
What Is True	101
When Peace Like a River	103
Your Love, My Lamp and Light	104
About the Authors	106
Acknowledgments	127
Other Works by the Contributors	136

Introduction

Let us share a story.

This is a story of hope and loss, of finding healing in the midst of pain and grief.

In 2023, Kanasy Yeager went up to the Nationwide Children's Hospital in Ohio to have surgery to remove a mass in her left upper arm that was the size of a butternut squash.

Skip to the new year. The mass in her arm started coming back, so she went back up to Ohio to get her left arm amputated. Thirteen days later, she had cancer removed from her lungs.

She healed and was better for two months, but then the cancer in her lungs began to come back in April. She considered going back to Ohio for surgery again, but ultimately decided against it because the spread was already extensive and more tumors would grow back quickly anyway.

Kanasy always looked on the bright side, never complained, was optimistic, and never lost faith in Jesus even amidst her pain.

Sadly, Kanasy went Home to be with the Lord the evening of June 8th, 2024.

She was healed, but not in the way we were wanting and praying. She is forever healed now. Now, she's not in pain and can rejoice in Heaven with both of her arms hugging Him.

During one of her last conversations on the YDubs Community, she said, "But death isn't the end."

Death feels like the end—the end of everything. Grief overwhelms us all. But, just like Kanasy said, death is not, and will never be, the end. It is only the beginning for the believer.

Even though Kanasy's earthly life has passed, her life continues on, and that is something to rejoice over.

We pray you will be blessed by Kanasy's life and words, and that the poems featured in this anthology remind you of that. God's not done with you, nor is He done with Kanasy and her legacy.

Blessings,
Erin Hylands & Rachel M. Adams

A Call To Adventure

By Autumn Acosta

A nation of houses like soup cans in a row
Complacently feeling secure in the flow
Icarius's opposite, too scared to fly
You're safe in the box you were cultured inside

You've built up your foundation on the bright sand
But complaining you are about drowning on land
What's stopping you from rowing out to the deep?
Relief comes in braving the change that you seek

What is the good of a ship that won't leave the shore?
Or one wary to move for fear of being sore?
Tired souls always stuck living in the past
Never realizing all of the life that they lack

These mountains need climbing, and it's up to you!
You can choose to keep your feet frozen or lace up your boots
Full or peril and failure is the way to the sky
But you banish success if you never dare try

Raise up the sail, pull the ropes, let us go!
I'm by your side on this narrow road home

There's fear in our hearts, but courage, too, I believe
They who call us dreamers are the ones fast asleep.

A Friend's Agony

By Autumn Acosta

The battle rages 'round
The storm beats at you with waves so tall
I can see the fire in your eyes
As you insist that you can take it all
Why do you deny the truth?
I want to fight for you

To me, the weight of your steps is plain to see
Yet you try to mask your struggle
The road is long, the hike is hard,
But still you hide your troubles
I'm right here, watching you labor through
Won't you please let me carry you?

Pride keeps you from the help you need
But it's not a shame to ask for help
The greatest obstacle you face
Happens to be yourself
Your deepest pain, it kills me too
Know that in a blink, I'd die for you

So I'll stand here patiently
Waiting for you to lean on me
My hand is out for you take
I promise I won't let you break
In the meantime I'll do all that I can do
I'll love and pray and live for you

America!

By Jaela Deming

Oh America, America!
Where are you?
Where have you gone?
Where did your Biblical foundation go?
When I look for you,
I find a nation who's run away
From her founding doctrines,
Who has apparently forgotten
That her only purpose
Is glorifying her Creator.
When I look for you,
I find a nation of evil,
Sexual perversion and violence,
School shootings and riots.
I find a nation who accepts
The slaughter of the unborn,
Of terrorism and lying politicians.
I find a nation of sin,
Who traffics and lusts,
Who allows government overreach.

Oh America, America!
I weep for you,
I mourn over your deeds
And dread your imminent destruction.
Why will you not return?
Repent, O you evil country,
You are doomed to destruction,
But there may yet be time!

Go back, I plead with you,
Back to a time,
Of justice and mercy,
Of liberty and principles,
Of morality and godliness,
Of happiness and prosperity,
Of life for all.
Back! Back I say!
Become once again
The nation you were made to be.
Return to your Creator
Before it is too late.

Oh America, America!
Your days are numbered.
Will you return to be
The beautiful rising sun
Your Founding Fathers imagined?
Or will you remain
The dying sunset,
Whose final rays of light
Are smothered by clouds
Of evil darkness?
You must choose quickly,
For destruction looms
On the near horizon.

Another Funeral?

By Leighton Opperman

i don't want to
go
to another funeral.
don't want to
just have to be the
distant relative, or the
friend who doesn't really matter.
don't want to have to stand there
and pretend
i wasn't closer
to them
than half the people there.
i don't want to cry
and wonder why
we don't
wear black and mourn
like we used to.
'cause in that moment,
i don't think i'll ever be the same.
And i won't.
please God, give me strength.
give us all strength.
none of us want
to stand there
and cry.
can we be
okay?
everyone's trying,
at least.

patting each other,
saying,
'it's not over yet. we'll keep fighting.'
and i wonder, how long
has it been since
i stopped fighting?
my tears are cold
against my face, and
even though i know it's not
over yet,
despair fills my heart.
how long has it been
since i
knew how to smile?
'Your kingdom come, Your will be done,'
i say, and hope
with clasped hands
and dreams made of satin
that i would be okay with His will
being done.
'cause right now, i'm not okay.
i raise my arms as
the tears roll down my face,
posing like Christian with his burden.
"take it,"
i scream,
"take my burden and fears!"
and pray
in wet, shrieking prayers,
that everything would be
okay.

A Petition

By Autumn Acosta

Fix my faults into your flourish
Change my pain into your poem
Model my cares into your clay
Carve my aches into your stone
Write my life into a story
Better than any I could make up on my own
Turn my sorrows to a song
That will make your glories known

Paint your laughter in the landscape
Add your own tears to the wood
Dab spots of sorrow in the background
And brush it over good
Spot upon the canvas, please,
Your love in bright red streaks
Turn this unworthy being
Into your masterpiece

May your mercy be a melody
Strum your spirit on these strings
Write your virtue into verses
And let a joyous refrain ring
Weave your heart into the harmony
Play your riff upon the keys
May your goodness echo in our souls
As this, your song, we sing

Use these hands to hold your pen
And scribble words across the page

Retelling in a different way
The truths that never age
Sow seeds inside my stories
Of all that's good and true
So that, in time, they can sprout and grow
Inviting others closer to you

A Prayer

By Margaret Pierce

Here I am, Lord
Take my life
Today I laid it down for You—
Live inside me
Holy One
Teach me only what is true.
Without You, I am
Dead, a slave
But You have set me ever free
I died today
And rose again
Because You resurrected me.
Now let me be
A living flame
To now proclaim
My Savior's name—
The One who free salvation brings,
Jesus Christ, the King of Kings.
Amen!

Beauty For Ashes

By Jessica Sprecher

Nothing but ashes
That's all that remains
The world's cast in gloom
When will sorrows end?
It seems quite so strange
That it's possible
To trade these sorrows
These sorry ashes
For something better
For, in truth, beauty?
Can one truly trade
Beauty for ashes?
How can it be so?
Why would someone want
All my burnt ashes
And give me beauty
In exchange for it
It seems mad, insane,
But it's heartfelt, true

Chiastic Lies

By Skylar Rivers

Have you lived? Yes, you've been living,
But, dearie, is that you?
Are you still living?
Are you slave, a puppet,
To your own sweet self?
Those lies you tell yourself,
You've taken self-esteem and dumped it.
Lately I've been quite forgiving,
But there's only so much I can do.
Lately you've forgotten how to be living.

Come To Jesus

By Margaret Pierce

Are you weary as you read this?
Do you long for peace and rest?
My Jesus' yoke is easy
And He knows and loves you best.

Are you lost and seeking guidance?
Do you long to find the way?
My Jesus is the Way to life
He authored every day.

My Jesus is the Shepherd
For the soul that's gone astray
He's the Healer, Light and Comfort
And His steadfast love will stay.

Come to Jesus, strong and kind
Gentle, faithful, true
Trust in His eternity
And let Him carry you

Conflicted

By Cadence E. Witt

I'm not much for people
But I can't stand to be alone
I let fear control me
Though Christ sits on the throne

I lock myself in my room to read
But say yes to every RSVP
When I look to God
I can see my beauty clearer
But I feel nothing but ugly
When I look in the mirror

I believe I am the greatest
Until I hear another's latest
I want to travel and worship
But I am afraid, I am as social as a hermit

I want to sing and play on stage
But am always glued to my book page
Extroverted, introverted
It changes from moment to moment
Too often feels like some sort an of opponent

There are times I feel free
Times I feel constricted
And though there is peace in my soul
In my mind, everything is conflicted

Consider It All Joy

By Erin Hylands

Consider it a joy—
A joy.
All things a joy—
All trials;
All tribulations;
But how?
And whither?
And why?
Am I fine?
Am I fine?
What is fine?
How can I
Consider it all joy
When it seems as though
My joy is lacking?
It is a joy that only
Christ can understand
Only Christ can give
And only through Him
Can I receive it.
So I consider it all joy
Because of Him alone,
The creator of my joy.

Courage.

By Autumn Acosta

Let me see your *courage*.

Let me see you laugh in the face of darkness
Let me hear you singing over the rain
Let me feel the strength in your weakness
Let me see you love despite the pain

Let me see your *courage*.

Let me see you fight when all odds are against you
Let me touch your hand, calloused from working hard
Let me watch as you stand up for the truth
Let me see the light as it shines through your scars

Let me see your *courage*.

Let me see you showing others that they're not alone
Let me look at you daring to climb mountains and slippery slopes
Let me know that you know that you're known
Let me see you clinging stubbornly to hope

Let me see your *courage*.

Darkness Is In Vain

By Leighton Opperman

At night I sit in the moon's glow,
I like to watch it wax and wane,
The stars twinkle a last goodbye.

I fight against the pain.
I violently swipe my tears.
I wish that my hurt would refrain
from dropping me into Dark and shadows
Into the night and chilled, cold rain.
I cannot stand this solitude,
I squelch my grief with such disdain,
You always haunt my memories,
My dreams a never ending chain.
I cannot break against the heartache—
I know your love will remain,
Your word in me echoes,
The darkness tries me, all in vain.

Dearest Friend

By Jaela Deming

Dearest friend of mine,
Though times may be tough,
Although life may beat you down,
Though the future is uncertain,
One thing you can know.

Dearest friend of mine,
Always remember this thing,
You're more loved than you know,
More precious than you realize,
And more treasured than you think.

Dearest friend of mine,
The Devil wants your soul
To make you slave to darkness,
Christ died to give you freedom,
But you must accept His gift.

Dearest friend of mine,
Will you submit to Satan,
Or will you choose life
As a fellow heir to God's kingdom?
You must choose for yourself.

Dearest friend of mine,
I know this is a hard topic,
And I ache at the very thought
Of damaging our relationship,
But I must speak truth – in love.

Dearest friend of mine,
Do not let shame define you.
Do not allow loss to shape you.
Do not let fear control you.
Do not allow Satan to rule you.

Dearest friend of mine,
May you find the peace you need.
May God bless and keep you.
May you feel His unconditional love.
My prayers are with you.

Death Defeated

By Jaela Deming

Even now O Lord,
I will trust You.
As fear grips many
And Death roars,
His grim victory cry
Over many lives ended.
But Death can't win,
Because I was bought
With the precious blood
Of the perfect sacrifice,
The Lamb of God.
Christ has defeated Death.
While Death will still,
Take hold of this,
Earthly shell of mine:
He has no eternal
Claim on the soul
Of this Blood Bought
Daughter of the King–
Only JESUS does!

Despair the Messengers
By Skylar Rivers

He just wanted silence, not this verbal violence,
This blasphemy, this hypocrisy,
This battle cry with no explanation why.
A call, a shout, no reason to doubt,
That warriors united shall remain beknighted.
A messenger, a league of them,
Come running back, all tired,
They came back.

"More messengers," they plea,
"That's all this world will need."
So the town followed suit.
A commonfolk, the wisest sage,
Knows more than that, that battles wage,
That men will fall, that wounds won't heal,
The messengers will know nothing but fear,
As they run back to share the tragedies.
He stays in town, and watches, soul down,
As foolish men leave the town to burn.

Dross

By Leighton Opperman

"Hope is just dross that demands to be purged,
From tarnished to dripping gold.
It'll hurt you, a mighty dirge,
Burning away grief, fear, and nightmares of old."
And yet it is a beautiful thing
Don't listen to what the world tells you, hope will ring
My blood screams, "Vengeance is mine,"
But even in pain, I know the truth
That for all of time
Vengeance isn't mine,
It belongs to the Fire that burns within me
To make me whole.
Oh, my soul, look and see
With hope, my broken, burned heart is full.
Must I measure my worth in gold,
Or can I weigh it in hope?

Eclipsed

By Autumn Acosta

I light my candle to show the way
But why can't I see its glow?
I wonder if out went the flame
So I bring my finger to the wick so I can know
The warmth of the fire's certainly there
But strangely, something isn't right
Why is my sight so thus impaired
That this candle seems to give no light?

Confused I decide to carry on
Stumbling my way forward
I wait for clarity to come with the dawn
But I trip and find myself in the dirt
Is this road some kind of curse?
I try to keep making my way
But the situation's getting worse
Anger mixes with dismay

My frustration then turns
To the lit wax in my hand
How on earth can it burn
But not light the way? I can't comprehend
Then I feel a warmth upon all my skin
And my eyes are opened wide
As realization suddenly sinks in
Frantically, I look around in surprise

I see the other light, shining brighter than the sun

How on earth did I not notice it before?
Fully engulfing everything and everyone
Now that I see it, I can never it ignore
It makes sense now why my candlelight was never seen
Looking back my way's made crystal clear
All the lights are eclipsed by this much greater thing
And I understand that it's always been here, drawing me near

Falling

By Anna Kailin Fletcher

I felt that I was falling
Into the dark unknown.
I heard His heart calling,
Calling to my own.

But His voice I did not want,
His call I did not heed.
I did not want Him in the front—
I thought that I could lead.

But He chose not to leave me
Although my head was strong.
He would not let me be,
And showed me I was wrong.

So now I live for Him,
For He's the LORD of Light.
My vision's ever dim,
But He is ever bright.

Flame

By Margaret Pierce

This light in me is blinding
And I love to let it burn
Fill the world up with its truth
Let all hearts to Jesus turn

Yet I live to please myself—
Love to live like I am mine
My darkness clouds this beauty
I forget to let it shine

Jesus, now I pray that You
Would cleanse my selfish soul
'Til I'm nothing but Your light
That makes the broken whole.

Friendship

By Autumn Grace

When we were young and free,
We built a kind of ship
And called it Oversea.
We chopped the wood and hauled the logs
And took them to the sea.
We raised the pennant, flung the flag
And set to sea, just her and me.
The skies were clear, the waves were glass,
The course: the shores of Truly Free.
We sailed that ship and lived our lives—
We thought it was a treasury.
The skies grew dark, the waves were large—
I grew scared, and she deserted me.
I lost that ship and lost myself,
While all alone she left me.
I found our port and swam on in,
Away from evil seas.
Now I know I need another ship,
Another 'her and me.'
To cross the waves and reach
The Land of Truly Free.
No one has ever crossed those waves alone,
Nor singly crossed the sea.
It wasn't possible to go alone
Across that dreadful sea
But as I stood and thought of ships,
It occurred to me
That I was scared to reach that land,
The Land of Truly Free.

But then I thought it through once more
And something occurred to me.
That there was Another
Who'd help me reach the Land of Truly Free.

Heartsong

By Ava Hope

My heart oft' sings a song
Saltwater coated my lashes
Ran down my face
Til' joy came dancing along

My soul oft' tells a story
I was chained to the floor
Mangled in darkness
Til' I was freed in glory

My mind oft' pens a poem
I bled a river of blood
From the canyon etched in my chest
Til' I discovered my home

Now silent I cannot be
The barrier has burst
The shackles were cut from my tongue
I will sing the song You have placed in me

Heavenly Maze

By Jaela Deming

A starry evening begins to appear...

Stars emerge to sparkle in the sky
Twinkling merrily above so high.
A crescent moon shining bright
Radiates a soft, luminescent light.
Restless animals cross the sidewalk path
Yawning as they savor a moonlight bath.

Each night out my window I gaze,
Viewing such a heavenly maze.
Enjoying God's beautiful creation,
Now reminding me of my salvation
In the blood of Jesus spilled for me
Nobility laid down, a servant to be.
God's grace bought for a price.

History

By Hazel Honegger

We are old and we are tired,
Tired and worn through.
We drag our feet on the path,
The way of history.

The way of ritual,
The way of tradition,
With peaks of discovery,
And dips of depression.

Through war and peace,
And pride and shame,
Through joy and fear,
The road's the same.

Onward, onward,
Never-ending,
Leading, leading,
Hard and bending,

Leading where?
No one can say.

We say it is a better place:
We hope it is a better place,
But the road is as old as we,
And we have not got there yet.

Maybe the young can tell you.

We are young and we are strong,
Strong and glorious,
We lift our heads and fight:
We forge our destiny.

We left ritual,
We left tradition,
We flattened discovery,
And filled in depression.

No war, no peace,
No pride, no shame,
No joy, no fear,
Our freedom's name.

Do not ask us where we came from,
Do not ask us where we're going,
Do not ask us what we want,
For we see all, and we want nothing.

We left the path, and we go nowhere.
We walk in circles,
Endless circles,
But they're our circles.

There is a path,
Another path,
A second path,
An older path.

I saw an old man walking it:
He said that he was walking it,
Living on this second path

Even while his feet were on the first.

I saw a lady walking it:
She said that she was walking it,
Living on this second path
Even while she stood among the young.

This path is strange,
The old are skeptical.
They say, "We cannot see this second path,
It is invisible.
Yet speak to those who walk it,
And they will say,
The path they tread,
Is clearer than our own.
But is sight not everything?"

The young laugh and say,
"This second path is folly and is old,
Yet they say they are wisdom and are young.
Both young and old has not been seen,
Ridiculous, impossible, absurd.
Is sight not everything?"

There is a spot upon the old one's road,
That has been touched by Something,
And all the zeal of the young,
Yearns for Something,
But they reject it,
For they reject all things.

The old are right,
The young are right,
And both are wrong.

> For this second path was born and has always been,
> Has died and will never end,
> Time is too small for it.

The Conclusion of the Matter: History repeats itself. Many are caught up in the constant pursuit of something better, a new technology, a new philosophy, a new way of life. Traditions die to traditions in this never-ending race. Many others reject this road, saying there is nothing worthy of pursuit. They say there is no greater meaning, that there is nothing new under the sun. In this they would be right, for even their proud words have been said before. And yet, the life, death, and resurrection of a single man, Jesus Christ, has managed to change the fate of the entire world. It is perhaps ironic that the only truly new thing is the oldest thing of all. And yet the very essence of this incomprehensible thing shows how the traditional old and rebellious young are one and the same in the ways that count, they both walk by their own strength. In their ignorance they are blind to the very thing in which they have hoped. History still repeats itself, but the difference now is that there is a choice, a second path, to be walked in a strength not our own. Jesus Christ has truly changed the course of destiny. Those who walk the second path find that for them the footfalls of history have been forever redirected heavenward.

Hold On Tight

By Autumn Acosta

Hold on tight, this is your story
This pain, this fight, is growing you to glory
I am the wind, and I am the light
I am the star leading you through this night
So hold on tight

I will be a sturdy rope to swing across the gorge
I will be the satisfaction when you're needing more
When you cross the narrow bridge, I will be the rail
I will be the rock of trust where others might have failed
So hold on tight

When words from others leave you sinking down to the floor
Know that I have found you completely worth dying for
To you my arms are ever spread out open wide
You always are and always will be precious in my eyes
So hold on tight

When you're cast down in the rubble I will help you build
When you're thirsting and in trouble, it's your cup I'll fill

Come to me you laden one, I will help you
stand
I will take the weight from you and offer you
my hand
So hold on tight

Hopeful or Hopeless

By Leighton Opperman

Hope is an Ornament
That some
People hang around with
Evanescent dreams,
Fully believing it will stay.
Until
One
Day,
All
Is
Lost.
Ornaments now
Receding,
Humanity troubled
Over it all,
Putrid stench of
Envy and
Loss now our only decorations.
Even through it all
Sunlight peeks in, a
Shining beacon of **HOPE**.

Hope in Five Senses

By Blessing Hope

Hope is a flower,
Fragrance wafting through
The perfumed air,
Sweetening.

Hope is a sunset,
Vibrant hues of pink and gold
That dance across the brilliant sky,
Soaring.

Hope is a butterfly,
Gossamer wings
That brush the back of your hand,
Stroking.

Hope is a stream,
Laughing and splashing
As water pours over the pebbles,
Singing.

Hope is a cake,
Honey against your tongue
As you bite through airy layers,
Savoring.

I Can't

By Leighton Opperman

"I can't!"
I yell into the wind,
Even though I know
That no one
Will answer me.
"I can bear the burden no longer,"
I shriek at the rain,
"I'm sick and tired of being strong."
Then, I open my mouth
And begin to scream, a
Long, howling scream that makes me
Feel like a monster.
I don't care.
I feel empty, and yet
I am so, so full,
And so filled up with
Anger
And this sadness that
Refuses to leave, no matter
How much I try to shake it off.
And it makes me
Feel numb,
But it also forces me
To be sick with emotions,
To choke on my feelings.
I wish I could
Throw my feelings carelessly across the room
Like everyone else does,
Yet it holds on to me, determined

To take me down with it.
But then I look into the drizzling sky,
And a rainbow emerges,
Dazzling me.
There is beauty in the pain.
There is hope in the morning.

Jasmine

By Alladene Grace Hadden

Sweet and pleasant scent
Drifting softly through the air
Landing on a breath

Graceful vines weave round
Lush leaves reveal their faces
As the sunshine beams

Soft and slender stars
Peeping out amidst the green
Are blossoms most fair

The day jasmine blooms
Is a day much awaited
And afterward missed

Joy

By Erin Hylands

Joy
Something that I lack
Joy
Something that I want
Joy
Something that I need
Joy
Something that I seek
Joy
Something that's a gift
Joy
Something that's a peace
Joy
Something that's from God
Joy

Keilah

By Anna Kailin Fletcher

The Philistines were mighty,
But David stronger still.
He heard you were in trouble,
And asked of GOD His will.

Then David went to you, Keilah,
To save you from the Philistines,
To prove that they were not
As mighty as they seem.

But King Saul heard of you, Keilah,
And of David with you there.
And David sought the LORD again,
Lest he be in a snare.

And GOD said you'd deliver him
To the country's king.
And he was up and out of you,
For Saul could surely sting.

But after all he'd done for you
You wouldn't even care
To save him, for you were afraid.
Keilah, we've all been there.

Lies

By Leighton Opperman

You told me I'd be okay–
You said there's always another day.

**THEY SEE YOUR FEARS
BUT NO ONE SEES YOUR TEARS**

You said you loved me–
You didn't even hug me.
You said we were sisters–
Back then my fear was but a whisper

**OH BUT NOW IT'S GROWING
YOUR ANXIETY IS SHOWING**

I watched you walk away–
I was the one that stayed.
I thought you would return–
My grief's a stinging burn.

**YOU ARE ALONE
INSANITY IS YOUR THRONE**

The lies in my head began to grow–
I was my own foe.
I threw away hope–
It was a slippery slope.

**NOW YOU'RE IN GRIEF'S
CLUTCHES**

THERE'S NO ESCAPING ITS TOUCHES

And as I cried,
I tried and tried
To imagine another reality,
One where I could see.

THAT'S NOT A THING
ALL YOU KNOW IS LONELINESS' STING

'But I'm not alone,'
Whispered a voice I hadn't known–
A morality in my head
Reminding me that hope wasn't dead

I AM THE VOICE YOU HEAR
ALL YOU ARE IS FEARS

But the pressing thoughts–
What if all wasn't lost?
What if this wasn't the end?
What if I'd see the sun again?

LISTEN TO ME
YOUR HAPPINESS WILL NEVER BE

But what if the loud voice is a liar
And the quiet morality something higher?

NO
THERE IS NO ESCAPE

But what if you're only a voice?
What if I have a choice?

**DARKNESS HAS YOU
YOU'LL NEVER BE NEW**

'SILENCE!'
And the thought was a shout–
I would kick the darkness out.
I wanted the sun–
Never again did I want to run.
And the voice tried to come back,
But I just screamed,
'YOU CANNOT ATTACK!
I KNOW THE LIGHT–
IT HOLDS ME TIGHT.'

Moonlight Dawning

By Alladene Grace Hadden

A beat
The tide comes rolling in
Waves gather round my feet
A tug
The foam is pulling out
A swift and smooth retreat
A sigh
Escapes between my lips
As tears slip down my face
A whiff
Of salty ocean air
Shares the same, sad taste
A light
Appears a long way off
Distant in the skies
A shift
Within my sorry scene
The moon begins to rise
A thud
I drop back on the sand
And gaze upon the sphere
A crash
The waves keep their routine
As if I weren't here
A sense
That something's different now
Beams spill toward the sea
A gasp
Now I can see the the path

That's coming to meet me
A skuff
I'm slowly standing up
My eyes bent on the light
A quake
As I step, shivering
Into the dreamy sight
A pull
That draws me nearer still
Onto the shining trail
A note
Like silver bells resounds
My rhythm-keeping tail
A burst
Of speed, I lose control
The tempo raises high
A surge
I'm filled with energy
As I go racing by
A thrill
Within my heart and soul
I see a silhouette
A hope
Of healing oldest wounds
Of airing out regret
A warmth
I fall into strong arms
And then begin to weep
A love
So strong, it spanned the countless
Miles of the deep

A beat
I never want to leave

But know that soon I must
A tug
We start to separate
It stings like broken trust
A sigh
From my companion comes
Worth a thousand words
A whiff
Of a familiar scent
The last goodbye offered
A light
Behind my turning head
Reveals the distant shore
A shift
The sky is tinged with pink
From where I was before
A thud
My first and heavy step
Back toward the beach
A crash
Waves hit the sand ahead
Now barely out of reach
A sense
That though I'm back again
My heart is somehow changed
A gasp
I turn and see the bridge
Do something very strange
A skuff
I back onto the beach
And in the nick of time
A quake
The moon-bridge falls away
A fractured, fading line

A pull
That forces me to look
Though I want to turn away
A note
Of firm finality
As night turns into day
A burst
Within my aching heart
Like something in me died
A surge
Of tears rise to my face
Releasing what's inside
A thrill
A presence covers me
Sudden, swift, and sweet
A hope
From my great Comforter
I slowly take a seat
A warmth
Cascading over all
Enveloping my bones
His love
That holds me through my grief
Says I am not alone

My King

By Jaela Deming

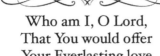

Who am I, O Lord,
That You would offer
Your Everlasting love
To a wretch such as me.

I have kept you
At an arm's length,
As a last resort
When time get tough,
Instead of turning
First to You.

I have tried to fix
Life on my own,
Carefully hiding my mess
Beneath a tidy mask,
Instead of running
First to You.

I have stuffed away,
Beneath a joyful smile,
The painful shame
That fights for hold,
Instead of giving it
First to You.

Yet still You wait
To rescue this lost sheep
Who has wandered once again,

From Your safe and loving
Fortress of refuge.

I don't know why
You have chosen me
As Your beloved daughter,
But today I dedicate
This life on earth
To serving You,
My King.

My Turntable

By Evelyn Harwood

Water to wine
Ugly to divine
Shame to glory
The sinner made holy
He is my turntable
He makes me able
Our darkness to light
From fear to might
Stressed to blessed
We were once the chaff
That blew with no purpose
Now we don't flee
We are the planted seeds
Rooted deep in water
Bearing spiritual fruit
We were the children of darkness
Now children of God fully zealous

Narrow Route

By Jessica Sprecher

The route isn't easy
It might be a little rough
Might be tougher than Mt. Everest
But the route leads to what we need
The route isn't easy
It is narrow but straight
It isn't wide like the other route
But take the route
That is narrow and straight
Because it leads to the Paradise
And Love that we need
Don't take the route
That is wide and easy
Because its end will lead
To pain and suffering
Beyond what we can fathom
So take the narrow route
It might be hard
But the end is Glory and Love
So take the narrow route
And don't give up

Next Steps

By Jessica Sprecher

I'm taking my next steps
It's a new season
I'm leaving harbor
I've been taught what I need to know
So I'm moving on

I shall look back on the past season
With great fondness
And perhaps I'll miss it
But I must move on

I can't be complacent
Though I want to be
I must move on

Start my new chapter
I need to take my next steps
I can't stagnate
I need to take my next steps
Despite the fact
That I would
Rather do anything
But that

Oblivious

By Margaret Pierce

Look at yourself.
Head down, shoulders sagging, plodding along
as if each step
Were a thousand miles long.
Oblivious
To the majesty
That pulses like the heartbeat of Creation
Through all, from the great
To the small.
What a fall.

Wake up!
Open your eyes!
Cast off your servitude to monotony
And see!

Run like the rain
Shout like the dawn
Rejoice in this world
That you're exiled from
Like a leper by choice
You are deaf to the voice
Of Creation proclaiming
The Kingship of God.

No wonder you say
It all happened by chance
Just a glance and you'd see!
How could such beauty be without purpose!

But no.
The whole world is aglow, and you
Blind yourself, wondering
Why your days are all
Night.

Open your eyes to the
Light!

Once I Looked Up

By Felicity Wales

Once I looked up at the sky,
Where stars reigned up so very high.
Once I looked down at a meadow,
Where a fox resided under the willow.

Twice I looked into the sea,
Where I saw the fish swimming free.
Twice I smiled up at a lark,
It's notes resounding through the park.

Thrice I glanced up at the trees,
The leaves rustling in the breeze.
Thrice I heard a musical note
From a girl in a red raincoat.

But in all those times I am around,
I remember I am homeward bound.
Naught to any place here on this earth
But to a place for my true worth.

Home to heaven, where God resides.
Home to heaven, where my Lord abides.
This is the sight I wish to see
And one to which I have the guarantee.

Once I asked the Lord to forgive me,
And He heard my sorrowful plea.
Once I wept o'er my lonely road,
But now I travel to my heavenly abode.

Once I looked up at the sky,
Where Jesus reigns up on high.
Once I looked down at the meadow
Where the lion rests peaceful under the willow.

Overwhelm

By Hazel Honegger

You're the Consuming Fire
Your Jealous Anger
Is known
Your Blinding Splendor
And Awesome Power
Overwhelm

You're the Great Creator
You're the Great I AM
You spoke, and all of nature
Came to be

You're the Ultimate One
You're Indescribable
Your justice
Is perfect
You're Undeniable
And yet You died for me
And yet You died for me

I am nothing compared to You
A speck of dust compared to Your Glory
Yet You see me
And You love me
And You gave it All for me
And You heal me
And You help me
And You lead me
And You say I'm Yours

And You say I'm Yours

And that is everything
I'm Your Daughter,
You're my Father
I'm the princess
You're the King
You are Holy
You are Awesome
I am not.

Oh Lord, Your love for me, it overwhelms,
Your love for me, it overwhelms.

Perfect Storm

By Owen Leo Snook

As rain clouds to dry earth
As a match to a cold hearth
As a stone to a dull blade
So the perfect storm was made

Sound filled the air, and my bones
With vibrant notes, undertones
It spoke to me pinioned words
Strange feathers from unknown birds

Echoes of days filled with light
Brightness has no end in sight
Light and love conquer the cold
Lies fail when the truth is told

As new rhythm to dead veins
As a balm to aches and pains
As a breeze to a still fan
So the perfect storm began.

Reassurance

By Autumn Acosta

I know that you've been broken
This life comes with fractures deep
There are days when you feel
You travel in one long tragedy

People left who should have stayed
Bitter words leaving such an ache
With hope you pray and wait and wait
But years go by without a change

I know, my dear, the way you feel
For you I cried in the garden
The weight of the world works to pull you
down
But I will help you stand
I bore the planet's pain upon my back
When I took the cross
I will share your burdens

Trade your pain--for my plan
Continue to wait--it's coming
Place your life--in my hands
If you hurt deeply, dear
Then you love deep, too
This is your story, and I'll
Share your burdens with you

Refuge

By Margaret Pierce

From deep within the shadows
Hissed a dark and potent dart
It snared my soul
And seared a hole
In my vulnerable heart.

It told me to be anxious
To give in to doubt and fear
It told me lies
Said not to rise
Told hope to disappear.

And I was captive to this wound
That shouted louder than God's song
It crippled me
And told me "See?
What God calls truth is wrong."

But the Healer of the soul
Who binds up wounds as deep as death
Gave me a sword
From which truth roared
And conquered darkness with a breath.

For the LORD gave us a spirit
Not of fear, but love and power
Self-control
He makes us whole
And His great name is like a tower.

So I will shield myself with faith
And wield God's Word as my great sword
I'll hope and pray
In Christ, the Way
And take refuge in the LORD.

Resilience

By Hazel Honegger

I fail daily, utterly—
I fail to speak, I fail to see,
I fail to walk the path I should,
Yet failure is not in me.

I fail daily, utterly—
Yet God's grace daily covers me,
New mercies rise with every sun,
Sin's lost its grip on me.

I fail daily, utterly—
But I'm more than my iniquity,
Chosen, loved, the Father's daughter,
In Christ is victory.

Shades

By Leighton Opperman

The world's a shade of gray tonight,
Blurry hues reflecting the
Effervescent mist in my eyes,
Wonder so quiet,
Only to brighten the next moment as my life
explodes in a
Reeling whirlwind of colors, and I often
wonder what it's
Like for those who only glimpse or
Dread the colors, the brightness only an
Inkling of a
Shadow because mysteries
Abound if you don't know what
Salvation is, or the difference between love
and
Hate.
And who are you holding your morals to, a
Dead idol that hoards skulls, or an
Eternal Father who never fails to hold you
close?
Only one of these can you choose, the
Father showing you the rainbow but the
Gray statues only showing you shades.
Rays of sunlight peeking into your vision
As morning arrives, you realize
You've made the right decision. This is Light.
These are Colors.

She Looked Back

By Sana Baig

As she stopped to catch her breath, she looked back. She looked back at the Sea of her Life.

And she saw how far she had come.

She saw the dark spots, where it looked as if a storm had brewed. She looked back at the wonderful spots where the waves rose and fell steadily. She looked back at the parts teeming with sharks and jellyfish. And she looked back at the part where the dolphins and seahorses played in the waves.

She looked back and remembered where she had been.

She caught her breath, and a giant wave of memories swept over her. The memories of fear while lightning flashed on the water. The memories of joy while playing with the dolphins. The memory of jumping over the calm waves. The memory of riding the high waves.

As she looked back and caught her breath, air filled her lungs. But this wasn't regular air. This air was different. It filled her with joy and a sense of adventure. It filled her with hope for the future. It filled her with love for the world. And it filled her with a deep yearning to see what the future holds.

As she stopped to catch her breath, she looked back.

And gained the urge to go forward.

Silence

By Margaret Pierce

In this wide open space
In this grassy clothed place
I'm in awe of the silence
That roars in the air
I can't stop to listen
Can't have it in full
Poured into my soul
In its powerful whole
It's too potent,
This stillness
That
Rides
On the wind
That
Hides in plain view
For when God met Elijah
He came not in flame
Not in earth's mighty quake
Or a gale, trees to shake
But He came
In a
Whisper.
A silence.
A breath.
And the first sound that signaled
Death's death
Was
A breath.
And the last sound that signaled

Free
Grace
Was
No breath.
Silence.

Sometimes

By Margaret Pierce

Sometimes
Creation's so stunning
I don't
Want to write
It down
Don't want to bottle it up
Into the confines
Of lines
Don't want to take time
To rhyme
There's a season
For reason—
But not now.
Now's the time
To wonder
At the thunder
Stand in awe
At glory raw
Simply
Fill your lungs
With air
Simply
Make your heart
Aware
That all
You cannot comprehend
Into
Vivid being came
By the

One
Who knows
Your name.

Surrender

By Hazel Honegger

What do You want me to do, Lord?
Do You want me to let go?
Do You want me to keep going?
Lord, I really want to know.

Your ways seem so foreign—
Beyond all I can see.
But I will trust in You, Lord,
In the plans You have for me.

I long to see You clearly—
I want to know Your face.
But if I want to see You,
I must trust Your ways.

I surrender to You, Jesus—
I give You everything.
I kneel down before You,
And crown You as my King.

I don't know how many times
I'll pray this little prayer.
But I trust You know my meaning:
I long to know You here.

So, I surrender everything—
I give You the life I lead.
Take it away and lead me
Along Your path instead.

Tears

By Rachel M. Adams

Let those tears flow
Like a river flowing steadily
Water trickling down my checks

My body shaking
Crying frantically
And hyperventilating

Blowing my nose
Wiping my eyes
Crying frantically

Someone holding me
Helping those tears
Helping them stop

Or helping them fall
Praying that they stop
But they just keep coming

The Seashell

By Blessing Hope

A shell upon the ocean floor,
Nondescript except to One
Who treasures it with all its blemishes.

Yet who would value a seashell
As priceless beyond measure?
Who would take it up and polish it,
So that it shines for everyone to see?
Who would choose the one with flaws
When there are much more perfect ones?

A shell upon the ocean floor,
Nondescript except to the Perfect One
Who treasures it for its blemishes.

The Storm

By Margaret Pierce

I saw it from a distance
As it swept across the sky
As its edges foamed and furrowed
As it towered from on high
As it chased away
The pearly blue
Erased the sky's
Indifference, too
And lightning bolted crystal
And the thunder bellowed deep
And the velvet clouds stampeded
Like a flock of charcoal sheep
And they rushed into
Their waiting meal
And crushed the blue
With hooves of steel
And now it was among us
And the rain came crashing down
And the cold swept in with drama
Wearing lightning as her crown
Then all at once
The world was wild
But all the stunts
Were soon exiled
And soon the thunder ended
And the lightning was no more
And the downpour stilled and silenced
And it was stiller than before
And the sunset sailed

As colors grew
And the ones once paled
Now shone anew
And the silence left is golden
In the thunder's silver wake
And the colors are a towel
After charcoal's soaking lake.
It was mighty in its brief life here
But most generous in death
Just as Jesus' greatest triumph
Followed after His last breath.

The Whole World Is In Your Hands

By Hazel Honegger

If only we could always remember,
If only we could fully trust,
That what You say You'll do with power,
And that Your love is always enough.

If only sin would cease to bind us,
If only we could understand
That all good things are gifts from Jesus,
And the whole world is in Your hands.

We are limited,
And we are weak.
We're crying out,
We're on our knees.
Lord, give us grace,
Faith to believe.
Help us to trust
That You are King.
Lord, show us Yourself again,
Lord, show us Yourself again.

We are foolish people
With forgetful minds.
You're the Holy One,
The King on high.
That we forget You
Is to our shame,

When we live and breathe
By Your great name.

Yet You're the God of mercy
So the price You've paid.
You're the God of mercy,
So I wake each day.
You're the God of mercy,
So You show Your face.
You're the God of mercy.
So I can say
The whole world is in Your hands.

Even when we do not remember,
Even when we don't understand,
Still You reign with loving power,
And the whole world is in Your hands.

Lord, we have seen You always remember
When time's days have passed like grains of sand.
Then You will crush sin's binding power,
For the whole world is in Your hands.

This is Reconciliation

By Rachel M. Adams

What is this feeling?
This is reconciliation—
I am restored.

I am at peace.
This is reconciliation—
I'm loved so much.

He will restore me.
This is reconciliation—
Are you full of joy?

Yes, I am now.
This is reconciliation—
He's close to me.

I'm broken-hearted.
This is reconciliation—
He will fix my heart.

This is reconciliation.

This Monster

By Eliza Thompson

There is a monster in my heart.
A monster fed on terrors,
Bred on shadows of the past,
Awaiting the earthquakes of tomorrow.

There is a monster in my heart
With six heads, six horns, six eyes.
It lies in the caverns of demise.

This monster that lives in my heart,
It hunts, it bares its fangs.
Rearing its ugly head, it roars.

Eyes aglow, that dragon-beast whispers,
"When was the last time the sun shone?
How much goodness have you ever known?"

There is a monster in my heart,
Who scorns the day and awaits the night:
The night where shadows are all one sees.

There is a monster in my heart,
Who cries at every joy and
Rejoices at every anguish.

There is a monster in my heart,
Who makes me fear him:
The shadows, solitude, transparency.

There is a monster in my heart.
A monster of shadows, illusions, lies,
But at the end of the story, the monster dies.

Tirade

By Ava Hope

Tirade has bane of eternity.
Sharpened arrows:
Accuracy.
Is there no armor
Nor bandage
Passional
To embrace the
Cruor stream
Of punctured heart,
To pull the shaft
Up from the fount,
To stop the poison
Of anger's account?
I then recall the lay
I love to sing:
When all is pain,
All is well with me.
Your kindness is aid
Of eternity.
Your healing strength:
Divinity.

Violets

By Ava Hope

Why must the glass
Be shattered and flowers wilted
On the trodden path:

Delicate trampled to bleed in the gore
Of careless words unbridled?

Why must the water spill out and wet the dust?

What was a beautiful vase of violets is
Utterly demolished and
Seems beyond repair,

But the tender hands of kindness
Collect the broken pieces and
Slowly place them back together.

Reassembling takes time,
But in the end,
It becomes whole.

Still, there are scars that tell a story
And chipped glass that bring back
Recollections of the shattered state.

Nevertheless,
New flowers bloom and the
Mangled ones are tended to.

Old wounds and petals abashed
Are rendered to gentle care
And a grave,
Forgiven and left to the past.

So fix what has been broken and
Replant what has been torn.

Fill again the tattered vase so
The violets can thrive
Once more.

What Is True

By Margaret Pierce

I was given a book full of poems today
Grand works from poets a hundred years past
And it seemed that their work was much better than mine
Who knows if my scribbles and scrawlings will last?

But the truth came to cloak me
In confidence meek
And told me it's true
That I'm sinful and weak.

But God chose the humble
To bring down the proud
God chose the quiet
To drown out the loud

God chose the mute ones
To make known His song
And God chose the weakest
To bring down the strong

So what's grand doesn't matter on God's holy scale
Both the weak and the strong, He will use and make new
And what people might think doesn't matter to God–

What matters is simply I write what is true

When Peace Like a River

By Erin Hylands

When peace like a river
Gushes through me
It seems as though a shiver
Coursing through me

When peace like a river
Gushes through me
It makes me want to quiver
Shaking through me

When peace like a river
Gushes through me
It seems I'll never waver
Staying through me

Your Love, My Lamp and Light

By Emily Sweeney

When the sun ascends, painting colors in the sky,
I can feel Your presence, looking down from on high;
In the vast expanse above, where the stars align,
I know it's You, shining Your light divine.

You're the One who guides me in the night,
Your love, my lamp and shining light;
When the world feels heavy and my spirit is low,
I lift my gaze; Your light always shows.

Amidst the shadows, when darkness feels so deep;
Your light breaks through, waking me from my sleep;
With every gleaming ray, Your grace becomes my sight,
I'll follow Your lead, guided forward by Your light.

You're the One who guides me in the night,
Your love, my lamp and shining light;
When the world feels heavy and my spirit is low,

I lift my gaze; Your light always shows.

Even in stormy skies when the way is hard to trace,
Your light remains constant, no matter what I face;
With every step I take, I'm covered by Your grace,
Your love always leading me, illuminating every place.

You're the One who guides me in the night,
Your love, my lamp and shining light;

When the world feels heavy and my spirit is low,
I lift my gaze; Your light always shows.

About the Authors

Autumn Acosta

Autumn Acosta is in love with the Ozarks, where she has lived for almost her whole life. She is currently working on her writing ambitions while going to college full time at Missouri State University. In her free time, she enjoys anything that has to do with the Three Honored and Great Subjects (word, form, and song) and is always up for a bit of mischief and an adventure. She finds community at the organic vegetable farm where she works and at her church where she is blessed to attend daily Mass. Last but not least, she is obsessed with books, especially those by Tolkien or C.S Lewis. Oh, and coffee. Because books and coffee go quite well together, don't they?

Rachel M. Adams

Rachel M. Adams is a young teenager who uses her writing for the glory of God! If she is not writing, you can find her baking, running, reading, and spending time with family and friends. Rachel resides in the gorgeous Rocky Mountains with her family. She's also the co-fonder of Skillful Pen Press with Adeline Charlotte and Erin Hylands. To connect with Rachel visit her author site at: *https://authorrachelmadams.wordpress.com* or/and her blog *https://godsgotthepower.wordpress.com*.

Sana Baig

Sana Baig, a homeschooled teenager, lives in India, is a writer, a poet, and the founder of Behind the Writer's Desk (her monthly/weekly email list.) Sana's love for writing started at the age of six and has grown. She loves ballet, horse riding, piano, football (or soccer), and many more hobbies apart from writing. She is currently working on two novels, one a realistic fiction and the other a mystery comedy. Sana has traveled many places to in India and America and uses her experiences to write novels about transitions. She enjoys solving puzzles and reading books that make her laugh, drawing her to the genre of mystery comedy. Sana does school at home during most of the year, and in the summer, she loves to go swimming with her two siblings and spend the morning lying on her bed reading a book or drawing an animal. Sana aspires to become an author and hopes to impact her readers with her words. You can subscribe to her email list, Behind the Writer's Desk, at *https://behind-the-writer-desk.ck.page/0a6c5b418c.*

Jaela Deming

Jaela Deming was born and raised in Minnesota but has now made the hills and cornfields of Iowa her home of choice. Homeschooled throughout her academic career, she earned her Early Childhood and Youth Development Associate degree in 11th grade. She went on to complete her Bachelor's degree in General Studies with a double concentration in Literature and Early Childhood Education in 12th grade. Jaela discovered a love for writing at a young age and seeks to glorify God in all her stories. She considers herself a fiction writer who dabbles in poetry when inspiration calls. You can find her at *https://jjwrites4jesus.wixsite.com/faithfamilyfreedom*

Anna Kailin Fletcher

Anna is a young writer, singer/songwriter, wildcat lover (and cat mom!), artist, and a child of God. She's learning all about how to learn, cat care, how to improve as a writer and artist, and how to help tigers and cheetahs. She's homeschooled, a missionary kid in a country called Vanuatu, and blogs on two websites. She is so far unpublished. Anna knows when she has written through her allotted number of tedious days and yawned through her allotted number of sleepless nights, she will go home to be with her Heavenly Father and her LORD Jesus Christ to write Their praises forever.

Autumn Grace

Autumn Grace is an aspiring author who loves writing stories about strong family relationships as well as fantastical adventures and heroes. When not writing, she is usually drawing, listening to music, or hanging out with her family.

Alladene Grace Hadden

Alladene Hadden is an aspiring author and poet from Arizona. In addition to writing, she enjoys reading, acting, and exploring God's beautiful creation, all of which bring inspiration to her poetic style.

Evelyn Harwood

Although writing poetry specifically was something I was never interested in, that changed when I joined Youth and Government. One of the members with the help of others started a tradition that we still do today. Poetry Wars! A bracket style battle where after the first round all poetry is made live and teams for each round. These games showed me the beauty of poetry.

Hazel Honegger

Hazel Honegger is a young author who strives to write for the glory of God, aiming to present Biblical truth through fiction and poetry. She published her first novel, *The Cry of Oursay*, at the age of 16. She lives with her family in Ohio, where she enjoys homeschooling, running, crafting, and, of course, writing. Contact Hazel at *books.4.truth@gmail.com*.

Ava Hope

Ava Hope is a poet and young novelist with a passion for exploring the complexities of human experience through fiction and fantasy. Her storytelling journey began at an early age, sparked by a love for reading and a vivid imagination. As a dedicated Young Writer's Workshop member, Ava seeks to glorify her Creator and infuse her writing with messages of hope and beauty amidst life's brokenness. Her poetry has resonated with readers across various platforms, including her inclusion in the anthology "Life of a Writer," where her verses capture moments of introspection and wonder. When she's not spinning stories in the mountains of Colorado, Ava can be found hunting for Narnia in wardrobes, engaging with writers through her podcast, or drinking copious amounts of tea. Connect with Ava on her website, *www.avahopeauthor.com*, where she discusses all things whimsy, faith, and storytelling.

Blessing Hope

As a homeschooled teen author based in Prince Edward Island, Blessing Hope can be found exploring wardrobes and searching for secret passageways. When she's not off in magical worlds, she's working as a camp counselor or writing middle grade fairy tale fantasy. She is also a member of the Young Writer's Workshop.

Erin Hylands

When she's not reading, Erin Hylands can be found dreaming up her next story in spite of the notebooks full of half-finished ideas. She seeks to write for the One who created words because He alone deserves the glory. If you visit her, you might have a hard time getting a word in edgewise with her nine younger siblings following you. You can connect with Erin online on her blog that she shares with young author Cari Legere, *https://twofriendsonepen.wixsite.com/twofriendsonepen*, or her email list, *https://kannwriter.myflodesk.com/*, or on the publishing company she founded with Adeline Charlotte and Rachel M. Adams, *https://www.skillfulpenpress.com/*.

Lissie Laws

Lissie Laws is a young Christian writer who is in the midst of discovering what God has planned for her life. She is headed to Cedarville University to get her Journalism Major and is a graduate of the Proofread Anywhere program. She has self-published two stories and hopes to one day publish more stories and share God's word through them. She lives in a tiny Colorado town (not near the mountains) and has plans to take over the world with her best friend... as soon as they finish that one book they've been meaning to read.

Leighton Opperman

Leighton Opperman fell in love with dragons at a young age and never recovered. But now, instead of dreaming about them, she writes them. She lives in Minnesota with her family, two cats, and two dogs. When she's not trying to find a better word to describe the color brown, she's playing cards with her siblings, gardening, drawing pictures of her characters that don't turn out quite right, reading through her piles and piles of books, or daydreaming about future stories.

Margaret Pierce

Margaret Pierce is a popcorn-eating, pencil-losing, paintbrush-wielding purveyor of poems who loves alliteration almost as much as she loves similes. In everything, she seeks to make known the power of God and grace of Christ. Margaret lives in the Midwest in a big yellow house with half a dozen of her favorite people in the world.

Skylar Rivers

Once upon a time, there lived a girl, who we shall call Skylar. From a decently young age, she began writing tales of crazy sagas of fire-wielding princesses and flying cats, chocolate dragons, and tornadoes driving two friends apart. As she matured, she began to write less of those stories and far more stories of stubborn princesses and magical watches, formerly villainous baby dragons, and earthquakes driving two friends apart. Fortunately her writing style has improved from when she first started writing. Skylar is a girl who might say that she bounces between genres, but the truth is that she always comes back to fantasy tales and... interesting poetry. You can find her at: *skyriverwrite.blogpot.com*

Owen Leo Snook

Owen Leo is a world-weaver, cartographer, story-writer, coffee expert, and amateur miniature painter hailing from the forested mountains of Asheville, NC. After discovering a newfound love of poetry in 2022, he began sorting and stacking words together in new ways to build anthems, poems, and ponderings on various topics including time, places (imaginary and factual), decay, weather, internal musings, his many befuddling dreams, and most importantly, his Creator—the One who gives and takes away. At 17, he is currently working on a table-top roleplaying game called Squirrels Arcane, themed on light versus darkness in a mysterious fantasy world that could be described as a mix between Redwall and The Lord of the Rings. When not creating new words or imaginary civilizations, he can be found enjoying a good cup of earl grey.

Jessica Sprecher

Jessica Sprecher is a book nerd with a passion for almost all things literature, history, and God & faith. Her favorite genres to write are romantasy, fairytale reimaginings, and historical fiction. When not writing, you can find her curled up with a good book, dabbling in graphic design, participating in the YWW Community, or involved in some activity at her local church.

Emily Sweeney

Emily Sweeney is a young writer, artist, and entrepreneur who desires to show the light in the darkness, whether through her paintings, words, or just a smile. When she's not working on her latest writing project, she enjoys reading, blogging, spending time with family and friends, and learning all she can about horses and homesteading.

Cadence E. Witt

I am a born-again Christian who is saved by Christ's blood. I am a singer and guitarist up for hire and an aspiring book-writer who wants to write fun and adventurous fiction novels that are clean and godly. But, most of all, I want to travel America, singing my songs and spreading the Gospel as I learn more about Jesus and what He has in store for me.

Acknowledgments

Overall

Thank you to God, Who is the One who made this book happen.

Thank you so much to all the poets who put their time and energy into making this book a possibility. This wouldn't have happened without you!

We'd also like to give a shout out to Adeline Charlotte, co-founder and former marketing director of Skillful Pen Press. We miss you, girly, and we wish you the best in your future endeavors.

Autumn Acosta

I'm abundantly grateful for all of the people who have helped me grow as a writer and who have inspired my love of poetry. Particularly I would like to thank my family, my teachers at WINGS, and all of the friends with whom I've discussed the amazing power of words. Thank you all for putting up with me! And, of course, where would anybody be without the one whose words spoke creation into existence? May everything be to the greater glory of God.

Rachel M. Adams

A big thank you to my family and friends who inspire me and help me grow every single day.

Another big thank you to the rest of the Skillful Pen Press team, for getting on board with this whole poetry anthology—this couldn't have happened without you all. And, of course, this wouldn't have happened if not for the Young Writer's Workshop. To all the instructors and staff, as well as my friends on the YDubs community: you all have helped me grow in my writing and in my spiritual walk so much. Thank you so much to all the other authors in this book: Autumn Acosta, Sana Baig, Jaela Deming, Anna Kailin Fletcher, Autumn Grace, Alladene Grace Hadden, Evelyn Harwood, Hazel Honegger, Ava Hope, Blessing Hope, Erin Hylands, Lissie Laws, Leighton Opperman, Margaret Pierce, Skylar Rivers, Owen Leo Snook, Jessica Sprecher, Emily Sweeney, and Cadence E. Witt—this wouldn't be a book without y'all. Than you so much to Kanasy! I miss you so much and I can't wait to meet you in Heaven. And thank you so much to Kanasy's family! I'm so grateful that you let us include Kanasy. Your daughter was amazing and there won't be a time when I forgot about her and her legacy. Thank you so much Yeager family. And big thanks to you, reader! And a final thank you to God.

Sana Baig

Thank you to my family for always supporting me. Thank you, Young Writer's Workshop and the YWW Community for always encouraging me. I wouldn't be where I am in my writing life now without all of you. Thank you, Jessika O'Sullivan. You have taught me more than you will ever know, especially about creating relatable characters.

Jaela Deming

Many thanks to my family and friends who have supported me along my writing journey with their encouragement, honest feedback, and patience. Special thanks to my Mom for always being my best advocate and staunchest support, always reminding me to glorify God in all that I do. Also, to my sister Maleah and my friend MJ, both of whom I can always count on to keep me going when I'm discouraged or doubting my scribblings. Lastly and most importantly, to my Lord and Savior for His everlasting love and mercy towards me. I am truly blessed beyond measure.

Anna Kailin Fletcher

Thank you God and my Sunday School teacher for inspiring me to write *Keilah*.

Autumn Grace

Thank you to my Mom for sharing good poetry with me, even when I didn't want to read it.

Alladene Grace Hadden

Thank you to my crazy, wonderful family; you never fail to encourage me in my writing journey.

Evelyn Harwood

To the Kaiser's for the random things they inspire us to do.

Hazel Honegger

Thank you to our God, whose plans are always better. Thank you to our God, in whose sovereignty I have put my hope. Thank you to our God, whose foolishness is wiser than our wisdom. Thank you to our God, who is making all things new. Thank you to our God, who is the fulfillment of our pursuits.

Ava Hope

For my parents, the two people who inspire me the most. Thank you for everything. For the YWW Community—I don't know where I would be without you all, so thank you! For Jesus—You are the Author of my story and the Love of my life. I can't wait to see what adventures we go on next!

Blessing Hope

This is crazy! I'm being put in a poetry book! Thanks first off goes to God for the amazing writing talent He gave me. The thread behind my random stories and poems. The reason I'm pursuing writing as a career at all. I don't think words could express how grateful I am for all the gifts You've given me. Even though I generally write fairy tale fantasy, an odd part of my brain likes writing poetry, too, so thank you, Erin Hylands, Adeline Charlotte, and Rachel M. Adams for this opportunity. My parents, grandparents, and of course, brothers, were instrumental in helping me grow up, so thank you! My best friend Lily, you make my life awesome! I'm excited to spend the entire summer with you. We will win Cabin Clean-up every day! The reason I write is to give all you readers hope in tough times. When you read my poems, I hope (no pun intended!) that you will be encouraged. So many preteens and teens are writing despairing poetry and stories these days. I don't want to be one of them. What acknowledgement section would be complete without thanking you, readers? You help to make this book possible, and I'm so grateful.

Erin Hylands

My life got kind of out of wack in January, so big thanks to Rachel and Adeline for heading up this project when I was MIA. We miss you, Adeline, and we pray for you.
This is for my family, for continuing to love me in spite of myself.
For the Yeager family, for working with me on the introduction and dedication.
This is also for Jesus Christ, for whom I would be nothing without.

Lissie Laws

Thanks to my parents (Mike and Sue) for teaching me about the Lord, which lead me to write this poem. And thanks to my friend Cari Legere for sharing this with me!

Leighton Opperman

My poems were inspired by and written thanks to many people. Mom: thank you so much for caring about my writing and pushing me forward, and giving me the courage to keep writing. Dad: thanks for always pushing me towards my Heavenly Father. I hope that I honor Him with all my words. A special thanks to my writing buddies. You guys are the best and always pushed me to keep going with your enthusiastic notes about my poetry. Adalynn, Willah, Evers, Justus, and Haddon: You guys can be distracting at times, but you're the best siblings, and I love when you ask about my writing. Love you guys. And lastly, I'm so thankful to God for giving me my words and the means to write them down, and for being my closest friend.

Margaret Pierce

Thank you—
To God, the Author of life.
To Jesus, the Word in the beginning.
To the Holy Spirit, the Helper.
To Mom and Dad, my loving mentors and wise friends.
To Harold, for making me laugh.

To Imogen, for encouraging me.
To Walter, for reading.
To Lucy, for being.
And to you, dear reader—for doing what readers do best.

Skylar Rivers

To all the fantastic resources and teachers out there who have rekindled my hidden love for poetry. It is to you I owe this honor. And to Edward Bulwer-Lytton for the famous quote, "The pen is mightier than the sword."

Owen Leo Snook

My most heartfelt thanks go to my mother, a poet herself who always has an ear for my written ramblings; the Potter, to whom I am the clay to be sculpted; and to Bluebird—I must admit I wrote a good deal of this in an attempt to impress you.

Jessica Sprecher

First off, I want to thank my Lord and Savior Jesus Christ for being my strength and keeping me afloat in life. Thank You, Jesus, for helping me and giving me the love of writing. May my writing always be for Your glory. Second, I want to thank my mom, who is the best mom I could ever have! You have helped me so much with your encouragement, your editing and feedback, and with your driving me to the YDubs Retreat! I am very grateful for you! Third, I thank my friends from church who keep asking to read my work and are so encouraging. Here's some poems you can read! And finally, I want to thank all the people on the YWW Community who have encouraged me, helped me brainstormed, edited, and Alpha and Beta read my stories and poems. I appreciate you all so much, and I thank you from the bottom of my heart for all the feedback and advice! May you all never give up on your hopes and dreams, even when things get hard.

Emily Sweeney

First, I give thanks to my Creator, for all that He's done and given me. Apart from Him I can do nothing. Next, thank you to my family for all your help and encouragement in everything I put my heart and hand to. And, to a special friend, Viv... Thank you for your help on this project. I treasure our friendship so much.

Cadence E. Witt

Thank You, Jesus, for all of my talents that you have blessed me with and the tools to make them better for Your Glory. Thank you, Mom and Dad for always supporting me no matter how crazy or... concerning my ideas are. Thank you, little brother, for always being my biggest fan, for standing tall and wanting to protect me. Thank you, my bestest friend in the whole world, Juliann, for always being there to laugh with me and be a couple of crazy teenagers. You have no idea how grateful I am that God brought you into my life and I pray you never, ever leave it. And thank you, Rachel M. Adams, for being such a light and inspiration. I pray that you make it far in your writing and always keep your kindness. And remember the little people after you become a famous author. –Love, Cadence.

Other Works by the Contributors

A Global Run: A Short Story by Erin Hylands
Bricks of Deceit: A Short Story by Erin Hylands
Chasing After Butterflies by Rachel M. Adams
Come Alive: An Anthology by H.K. Searls and Erin Hylands (featuring Lori Scharf)
Fairy Tales Made Modern Volume 1 by Erin Hylands
Faith of Four Seasons by Erin Hylands and Honora Reese
Mary, Queen of Scots: A Shakespearean-Style Play by Erin Hylands
Poems, Prose and Verse: The Life of a Writer by Erin Hylands and Eowyn Bolivette (featuring Ava Hope and Jessica Sprecher)
Shards by Savannah LeBlank (featuring Erin Hylands)
The Christmas Collectors Volume 1 by Rachel M. Adams, Erin Hylands, Cari Legere, and Angelica Steele
The Cry of Oursay by Hazel Honegger
The Young Writer by Erin Hylands
With Eyes of Blue by Erin Hylands
Who You Say I Am edited by Erin Hylands (featuring Erin Hylands and Rachel M. Adams)

Milton Keynes UK
Ingram Content Group UK Ltd.
UKHW030635071024
449371UK00001B/47